hot scottish summer

Emma Bray

chapter **one**

Ivy

I take in a deep breath, inhaling the salty sea air as I marvel at the beauty of the majestic waves crashing upon the shore. A light breeze makes me shiver and I pull my jacket closer around me.

Summer in Scotland isn't what I would call summer weather. It's barely sixty degrees here–not overly cold, but not warm enough to warrant a bikini. I glance across the beach, noting that it hasn't stopped the natives from sporting their swimwear. Bikini-clad bodies and naked male torsos scatter the shoreline. This is probably as high as the temperature gets on this little isle, so I guess it's warm for the locals. Not for me. I'm used to ninety-plus degrees.

At least I'm not bundled up like an Eskimo. I'm wearing a pair of shorts and a tank, but I have my lightweight jacket to help ward off the chill from the wind.

I feel a thrill of excitement bubble through me. I still can't believe I'm here in Scotland. It's like a dream come true. I pinch myself for the hundredth time to make sure I'm not dreaming.

I've always wanted to travel the world and see other countries, but this is the first time I've been outside of the US. My aunt flew me over here for my high school graduation present. I've only seen her in person a handful of times when she came to visit my mother and me in the States, but even though we haven't spent that much time together, I'm incredibly close to her. She's been there for every big moment of my life. We Face-Time almost every day, and I swear I'm closer to her than I've ever been to my mother.

Aunt Sadie gets me. I'm able to tell her things I could never tell my mother. Like how my real passion lies in writing. I've always been a bit of a bookworm, and my love of reading translated into writing. One day, I realized I didn't just want to read the stories that captivated me so much. I also wanted to write them.

So I've been writing in my spare time for years now.

While my peers were riding around after school or playing sports, I had my trusty little spiral notebook to jot down ideas and plotlines. Call me a nerd, but there's something about the glide of a pen over paper that enchants me. I know I could churn out more words on a laptop, but I like the nearly forgotten art of handwriting. I like to feel the words flowing from my fingertips. There's something so magical about it. I haven't published anything. It's just a little hobby of mine.

I just turned eighteen a few days before my graduation. I was the youngest kid in my class. Everyone else was already eighteen when they started senior year of high school, but that was okay with me. The only benefit of turning eighteen was making it legal for me to buy a lotto ticket or vote. There wasn't a presidential election this year, so it's not like I missed out on that, and it's not like you can buy cigarettes or alcohol when you're eighteen.

A grin pulls at my lips as I remember where I am. I'm in Scotland, and the legal drinking age here is eighteen, so if I want to try a sip of wine, I'll be well within my rights to do so. I know Aunt Sadie will be more than willing to treat me like an adult and let me take a sip of her table wine at dinner. Sadie has always indulged me.

My smile slips when I think about how my mother would disapprove. I know she loves me, but she worries so much. She wants better for me, and I get it, I really do. She doesn't want me to have to scrape and struggle like she did as a single mother, working whatever job she could find to put food on the table.

When Mom found out I have an aptitude for numbers, she started pushing for me to major in accounting. We don't have the money for me to go to college, but I was lucky enough to get a valedictorian scholarship, so I'll get a full ride. Everything paid for. I'd be an idiot to turn that down, and Mom is right that a career in accounting is flexible. I could work for any type of company or become a CPA and start my own business. The possibilities are endless. People always need accountants, so it would be a sensible, smart choice.

So, why does my stomach knot into a ball of dread when I think about sitting behind a computer screen and staring at spreadsheets and ledgers all day?

I know I'm good at accounting. I took Accounting I and II in high school, and I aced them. But nothing gets me more excited than watching words flow onto the page.

I bite my lip as the wind tousles my hair. I placate myself with the knowledge that I can take writing and literature classes as my electives in college. I'll keep my writing as a hobby. My little secret passion. Something just for me.

But in reality, I know I won't have time to write when I start college. I'll be too busy keeping up with my classes. And when I graduate and get a job in the real world, will I ever write again? Or will my passion be filed away into a box of broken dreams?

"Girl, what are you doing with that jacket on?" Aunt Sadie comes out onto the veranda wearing nothing but a modest pair of shorts and a tank top.

Aunt Sadie may be in her forties, but she looks as if she's in her late twenties at most. She's taken good care of herself, and she's one of those people who age beautifully.

"I guess it is a wee bit chilly," I say with a smile.

She laughs at my use of the Scottish word "wee." Even though Aunt Sadie grew up in the States with my mother, she came here shortly after they graduated high school. Aunt Sadie was always more like me. She had that wanderlust and urge to travel. She fell in love with the land here and said she felt a connection to it deep in her soul.

I suppose that's not too surprising since Scotland is where our heritage lies. All our ancestors were Scottish, so it's in our blood.

I certainly understand her sentiment as I take in the rolling green hills and the rocky beach below. I feel at peace here. It's like a calmness is settling in my bones.

I push all my worries and thoughts about college and my future away. I'm only here for a week of freedom before I return to reality. I'm not going to waste my time brooding over my future.

This is a once-in-a-lifetime vacay, and I intend to enjoy every second of it.

chapter
two

Sean

"Thanks for taking us out!"

"No problem." I smile and wave goodbye to the couple as they climb out of my boat.

Today was a good day. The fish were biting, and the tourists get to go home with a good catch.

One thing about being a charter guide is I can't control the weather. I always make sure to tell people that upfront. You don't get your money back because the fish don't bite.

I've been telling my boss, Deacon, that we should offer something different on the days when the fish don't bite. Like a tour package where we ride them around in the boat to different spots on the island. Maybe provide them with an informative historical tour.

He shoots all my ideas down, stating that it's his business and he'll run it the way he wants to. The problem is, he's been running it the same way for the last thirty years.

But times are changing.

I finish tying the boat off at the dock, thinking how I'd love nothing more than to own my very own charter business. But Deacon's been good to me. He took me in and taught me everything I know, so I can't betray him like that. It wouldn't really be a betrayal to start my own business, not in my mind, but Deacon would see it that way. If I split from him, I would become his direct competition and that would put our patrons in a difficult position because they'd have to choose whether to stay with him or go with me.

No. Deacon's been too good to me for me to stab him in the back like that.

But why can't he see I'm just trying to help him with my suggestions? I know we could triple our business if we changed a few of his archaic business practices.

I straighten and run my hands over my head to smooth my shoulder-length brown hair out of my face. Ma is always telling me I need to cut it, that I look like an old-school Highlander, but I don't have time to be sitting in a barbershop every few weeks like some pansy. I'm an outdoorsman.

Still, when the wind whips it in my face like this, I wonder if my mom isn't onto something. It might be easier to cut it all off.

I usually keep it tied back, but I lost the tie riding in the boat today. I rummage through my tackle box and find a worn piece of rope. It'll do. I quickly tie my hair back at the nape of my neck. The wind is whipping something fierce today.

When I finally get the blasted strands tied back, I look up—and damn near fall over at the vision before me.

My god, I'm looking at the most beautiful little lass I've ever seen. The wind is whipping her blonde hair back behind her, and it dips down below the hem of her shorts when she throws her head back and laughs. Those peals of young, feminine laughter float over to my ears. The sound is enough to make my heart skip a beat.

I step off my boat and stare in her direction as if I'm spellbound—and maybe I am because I've never had this type of reaction to any woman before.

She's walking along the shoreline with Sadie Summers, the woman who owns the house right on the beach. I'm instantly intrigued and want to know who she is. The isle isn't very big, and I know I've never seen this woman before, so she must be visiting. We get tons of tourists this time of year.

She's wearing a pair of sunglasses that shield her eyes from my gaze and I want to get closer to her so I can discover what color they are. Something tells me they're blue. But are they the robin's egg blue of the sky or the deep sapphire blue of the ocean? My heart thumps rapidly in my chest with the need to find out.

She's a tiny little thing, shorter even than Sadie who doesn't stand very tall herself. Despite how petite she is, her legs seem to go on forever in those denim shorts she's wearing.

I curse the jacket that keeps me from seeing more of her body.

I'm not some horny pervert lusting after the new girl on the beach. No, this is something deeper. It's like the moment I laid eyes on her and heard those gentle peals of laughter floating over to me, something clicked into place inside me.

Whoever this girl is, I know without a shadow of a doubt that she's meant to be mine. I've never considered myself a dreamer or one of those men who's got his head in the clouds. I've never thought about whether I believed in fate, but it's like I've had some sort of epiphany—like those people who suddenly come into religion and just *know*.

One look at this girl, and I suddenly believe in her. Every instinct is telling me to go over there and introduce myself to my future wife when Deacon comes striding out of the office toward me. When I say office, I mean the little shack he sits in during the day to book appointments.

"Sean! I need to have a word with you," Deacon barks out by way of greeting.

"Not now," I tell him without taking my eyes off my woman.

I hear the scowl in Deacon's voice even though I don't see it. "Dammit, Sean! Yes, now."

I ignore him and continue to watch my little lass. She looks so dainty and delicate, and my protective instincts surge to life.

I'm jerked from my reverie when I feel a sharp tug at the back of my head.

I round on Deacon with a growl but hold myself back from smashing a fist into his face. And that's only because he is who he is. Although Deacon's not quite old enough, he's like a father to me. He's the only mother-fucker on this entire island who can get away with something like that.

"What the fuck, man?" I demand irritably.

"I wanted to make sure you're going to the bonfire

tonight. It's a great advertising opportunity. There'll be plenty of tourists there."

I turn back to find my little lass and panic when I don't see her or Sadie anywhere.

I grit my teeth, my jaw ticking. Damn. Deacon caused me to lose them, but then his words register in my mind.

The bonfire tonight. Sadie never misses the bonfires. With any luck, she'll bring her little friend along, but even if she doesn't, I'll find a way to find out who she is.

"Yeah, I'm going," I grunt at Deacon. My thoughts are a million miles away from work and advertising, concentrated on the girl I've fallen in love with at first sight.

Deacon raises an eyebrow at me like he doesn't believe me.

"I wouldn't miss it for the world," I add, and that's God's honest truth because if it gets me closer to claiming my woman, I'll be there.

I'm antsy and impatient for the rest of the day, pacing around my little cottage just waiting for nightfall when I can go to the bonfire and see her. Swear to God, I'm worse than a high school boy on his first date. It's like there's an itch under my skin, and she's the only one who can scratch it.

I never arrive early but I'm one of the first people at the bonfire. Deacon makes me come to these events to pick up new customers. When he finally arrives, his eyebrows arch in surprise to see me already here. No doubt, he was expecting to drag me here like he usually does.

I ignore my boss, and eagerly scan each new arrival, looking for my woman. My stomach knots with tension when we're an hour in, and I still don't see my little lass or Sadie. I have half a mind to head over to Sadie's house and demand to know who the woman is and how I can get in touch with her. They'd think I was a madman, and maybe I am because I feel like I'll go insane if I don't find out who she is—and soon.

"What's gotten into you?" Deacon asks, peering up at me.

"I don't know what you're talking about," I mumble, my arms folded over my chest as I scan the beach.

My boss raises an eyebrow at me. "You're more uptight than old Mrs. Miniver." He's referring to the town prude, the little old lady who always seems to have a stick rammed up her ass.

Normally, I'd give him a shove for his teasing, but I'm not in the mood. He's right, though. Every muscle in my body is stretched taut and my nerves are on edge as I wait impatiently for my next glimpse of the pretty little lass I saw on the beach earlier today.

"Here, have a beer." Deacon hands me a lager.

Yeah, I guess I could use a drink. Maybe it'll help calm my ass down. I grip the bottle by the neck and take a long pull, my eyes roaming the area around us. I'm four beers in with Deacon when I finally realize she's not coming. Neither of them is.

My shoulders slump and a dark cloud settles in my chest. Why did I wait so long to take action? It's way too late for me to knock on Sadie's door. Fuck, I should have gone earlier. I could've come up with some excuse to drop by if I'd acted on my initial impulse. They'll think I'm crazy if I drop by this late at night demanding to know who she is.

Deacon is getting well into his cups. He switched from beer to whisky a couple of rounds ago. The moron should know that's going to make him sick. Beer before liquor and all that. But there's no telling him anything.

I give him a clap on the back before letting him know I'm heading out. I've made my obligatory appearance and spoken to the few people who asked about charters, and now I just want to go back to my place and go to sleep.

I need tomorrow to hurry up and arrive because come hell or high water, I'm going to find out who my little lass is.

chapter
three

Ivy

"Get up, sleepyhead!" Aunt Sadie's voice says right in my ear.

I blink my eyes open. I groan as she hops off the bed and flings the windows curtains open, flooding the room with bright sunlight. I hold my arm over my eyes as I struggle to adjust to the sudden brightness.

"Come on! Up, up, up! I've got something fun planned today!" Aunt Sadie says in a sing-song voice.

It's much too early for her chirpiness. "Aunt Sadie, I'm supposed to be on vacation. I'll be getting up early every day soon enough when I'm going to class. Can't you let me sleep in?"

She laughs in response. "You can sleep in tomorrow. Trust me, you won't want to miss this."

I peel an eye open and look at her curiously. "What is it?"

"You'll see," she says with a wink. "Make sure you bring your jacket," she calls as she breezes out of the room to leave me to get dressed.

That comment has me more curious than ever because Aunt Sadie has been making fun of me for wearing my jacket ever since I got here. Now she's advising me to bring it with me. What does she have planned?

I'm mid-shower when there's a knock on the bathroom door, followed by Aunt Sadie's muffled voice. "Make sure you wear your bikini underneath your clothes!"

I let out a laugh. She's sending me so many mixed signals. A bikini yet a jacket. I have no clue what she's up to.

I finish my shower and join Aunt Sadie in the kitchen. I ultimately opted for a simple pair of denim shorts and a tank top with my bikini beneath as instructed.

I throw on my jacket as Aunt Sadie fixes us a quick fruit and yogurt parfait for breakfast.

We chomp it down, and then she's ushering us out

the door, pointing to her Apple watch. "Come on! We gotta go!"

She leads me past the car and onto the beach. We can't be going far if we're walking.

It's early so there aren't many people on the beach yet. The air is crisper than during the daytime, and I inhale deeply, loving the freshness.

Aunt Sadie leads us over to the docks where several boats are sitting on the quay.

"Aunt Sophie, what—?" My question dies in my throat as a man straightens up in the boat. Dear Lord, he's huge.

He steps down out of the boat, towering over us, his eyes pinned on me the entire time.

He's not wearing a shirt, just a pair of swim trunks. His wild brown hair brushes the tops of his shoulders and he has a light beard. Not a full beard that some men wear, but more than stubble. His eyes are a stunning emerald green that rivals the rolling hills here in Scotland.

My god, the man looks like he stepped right off the cover of one of those racy historical romance novels.

My cheeks color as his intense gaze lands on me. My breath catches, and I tingle all over.

Who is this man? And *man* is the correct term. He's the epitome of the word. His chest is strong, and the muscles in his arms bulge as he moves. My eyes trail down his stomach, taking in the washboard abs. My blush deepens and I look away before he sees me shamelessly ogling him.

I've never been good at judging ages, but this man is older than me—maybe late twenties. He has an aura of worldliness, confidence, and experience.

"Hi, Sean!" my aunt Sadie chirps happily, oblivious to my plight.

The man doesn't even glance at her. He's still staring at me, his look so intense, it's slightly unsettling.

"You're my morning guest?" He directs the question at me.

Sweet baby Jesus, I almost melt right there on the spot at the sound of his voice. Rich and deep, it's a beautiful timber with a rolling Scottish brogue. I can't help but imagine how it would sound if he whispered it in my ear.

I bite my lip, and those green eyes flick to my mouth where I'm worrying the flesh between my teeth. His nostrils flare, and his eyes seem to darken.

I release my lower lip from my teeth, and he finally tears his gaze away from me to look at Aunt Sadie.

"Yep!" she confirms happily. "I booked it with Deacon yesterday. Didn't he tell you?"

"No," he answers, his eyes flicking back to me.

Sophie's phone buzzes and her face lights up as she looks at the screen. "I'm sorry, Ivy, but I have to take this."

"Ivy."

His deep voice speaks my name softly. The way he says it, like he's claiming it and making it his own, sends a shiver down my spine.

My aunt finishes her call, unaware of the tension crackling between the huge Scotsman and me. "That was work. We've been trying to sell this one property for so long, and we've finally got somebody biting. They want me out there immediately to show it."

My aunt sells properties over here in Scotland. That's how she makes the big bucks.

"Oh, no problem. I can find something to do around the house," I tell her, assuming we're going to reschedule. Why am I equal parts relieved and disappointed?

"No, no, no!" She holds up her hand. "You go on the charter with Sean. He'll take good care of you."

I glance over at the big, burly Highlander, my heart tripping in my chest at the thought of being alone with him. It's not that I fear he would hurt me or anything. I'm not getting those vibes from him at all. I'm afraid I'll be awkward and make a fool of myself. I'm already flushed and tongue-tied in his presence. Plus, I have zero experience with men.

"You got that right," he rumbles in that deep voice. "I'll take good care of her, Sadie. She's in good hands."

Aunt Sadie beams at him before she pulls me into an impromptu hug. "You'll have fun, dear, I promise. Sean is the best." She gives Sean a wink before she takes off toward her house.

My knees have turned to jelly, and my heart is hammering in my chest as I watch my aunt go, leaving me alone with this big, hulking man.

I swallow nervously and turn around, craning my head to look up at him. His eyes are pinned on me with that startling green intensity. "Are you ready to go for a ride, lass?"

My cheeks flame at his words. There's nothing wrong with his words, but the way he says them, it's like he's ascribing some other meaning to them.

Stop it, Ivy, I mentally chide myself. Get your mind out of the gutter.

He holds out his big hand to help me up into the boat. I hesitate a moment before I place my hand in his, but when his big, warm hand clamps around mine, I know I've hit a turning point in my life.

chapter
four

Sean

The sensation of her tiny hand in mine sends fire rushing through my veins. How is it that one innocent touch from this tiny woman is enough to make me insane with lust?

Ivy. My little lass.

I can finally see her eyes, and I was right. They are blue, but they're the most startling cerulean blue. My imagination didn't do them justice. They're framed by thick dark lashes, and she has the lightest smattering of freckles on her pretty cheeks. With her blonde hair and blue eyes, she's the purest thing I've ever seen. I can't wait to dirty her up.

"How old are you, lass?" I need to make sure she's of legal age before I take her out on my boat without adult supervision. It's company policy, but I'd be lying if I said I wasn't asking for an entirely different reason. I have purely ulterior motives for wanting to know if she's legal or not.

My stomach knots at the thought. If she's not already, it's going to kill me waiting for her to turn eighteen. It would be just my luck to finally meet the woman who's meant to be mine, only to end up having to wait for her to keep my ass from getting thrown in prison.

"Eighteen," Ivy replies.

I almost fall to my knees in jubilation at her answer. Thank Christ.

I clear my throat as I lift her onto the boat and then jump in behind her. "As you heard from your aunt, I'm Sean, and I'll be your guide today."

"What exactly are we doing?" she asks as she peers up at me curiously. The wind catches her hair and blows it into her face, but she captures it, holding it in one hand. "I'm sorry. My aunt kind of sprung this on me this morning, so I don't have a clue what we're supposed to be doing."

There goes that pretty laugh again. My chest tightens at the sound, and I rub the spot absently. Swear to God this precious girl and her melodic giggles are going to be the death of me.

"I'm a charter guide. I usually take people fishing. But we don't have to fish if you don't want to," I add quickly. "I can just take you on a ride in the boat."

I know fishing isn't for everyone. Deacon only wants us to offer fishing charters, but if my little lass wants to do something else, then that's what we'll do.

Her face breaks into the most beautiful smile I've ever seen. I swear it's like sunshine breaking through the clouds on a rainy day.

"I've never been fishing. Can you teach me?" She looks up at me with big innocent eyes.

Can you teach me? Those words coming from her sweet mouth have my blood traveling south.

Fuck, yes. There are so many things I want to teach you, little girl. Thank God she's eighteen. I'm twenty-six, so I'm not quite a decade older than her. But I wouldn't care if I was twenty years older than her. This girl is it for me. I feel it deep in my bones.

"I'd love to teach you." My voice comes out low and gravelly.

A pretty flush stains her cheeks. Everything I say to this girl comes out dripping with innuendo, but I can't help it. That's where my mind is. And it's not just about her body or that I'm horny. It's her. I want her. All of her.

I grab a life jacket and walk over to put it on her. I normally hand people their life jackets to put on themselves, but I'll take any excuse to touch her. I slip it over her shoulders and cinch it up in the front, letting my fingers brush over her through her clothing.

We're so close that whenever she looks up at me, I can see every fleck in those ocean-blue eyes. I take the utmost care in buckling her into the lifejacket because she's the most precious thing I've ever had on my boat. I don't want to chance any harm coming to her. Do I imagine her sharp intake of breath whenever my fingers brush over her neck?

My eyes flick down to hers, but she looks away quickly. My body hums with the need to kiss her, to claim her right here and now. I bite the inside of my cheek to keep from doing so. She doesn't know me, and I don't want to scare her but damn it's going to be hard keeping my hands to myself.

Yet, I'm excited at the thought of having her all to myself, to talk to her and learn more about her. But first, I need to get her to a more discreet location. I want to whisk her away to a place where it's just the two of us. No beachgoers or tourists to distract us. Just her, me, and the water.

"You ready?" I ask her as I settle down behind the wheel of the boat.

She gives me a wide smile and nods her head.

"Here." I toss her an extra pair of sunglasses. It's always a good idea to wear a pair of shades to protect your eyes from the wind.

"Thanks," she says as she puts them on. "I forgot mine this morning."

There it is again. That little giggle I'd give my left arm to hear every day for the rest of my life. And she looks too good with my sunglasses on. Seeing her wear something of mine gives me a sense of primitive male satisfaction. My cock hardens just thinking about how she'd look in one of my T-shirts.

I put the boat into gear and tear off through the ocean. I know where I plan on taking her. Not only is there great fishing, but it's my special place where I go when I want to be alone to think. Taking her there and sharing that part of myself with her feels right.

I can't wait to see what she thinks of it.

chapter
five

Ivy

I probably look like an idiot with this huge smile plastered across my face, but I can't help it. This is exhilarating! The wind whips through my hair, and I see now why Sean gave me sunglasses. It was incredibly thoughtful of him because they do protect my eyes from the wind. Plus, they cast everything in that whimsical amber glow, making everything look more vibrant. I glance over at Sean. His skin looks even tanner through the lenses, and I admire the way the muscles of his arms bulge as he expertly maneuvers the wheel of the boat.

He grins at me when he catches me smiling at him,

and my heart does a little flip in my chest like a dolphin leaping up out of the water.

He has such a beautiful smile, and he looks too damn sexy in his sunglasses with his brown hair whipping out behind him. I never thought I was one of those girls who was into guys with longer hair, but it works on Sean. It's untamed and gives him a wild look. He could be a scary-looking guy, but I feel completely safe with him—even if I am more than a little nervous about making myself look like a fool in front of him. I mean, the man is gorgeous. He probably has women hitting on him all the time. He probably has a girlfriend—or a wife.

That thought sobers me. I don't want to simper over him, especially if he's taken. And what am I even thinking about? If he's taken? It shouldn't matter to me one way or the other because I'm only here for a week. I can't afford to fall in love, and long-distance relationships never work.

Oh, my god, what's wrong with me? Why am I even thinking about relationships and love? Neither has ever been at the forefront of my mind. I look back out over the water and try to calm my racing heart and thoughts.

The boat finally slows as we near a tiny island. My curiosity is piqued when we pull up to the mouth of a cave and Sean skillfully maneuvers us inside. He moors the boat on the shore and ties it off to a nearby tree just outside the cave.

"Here we are, little lass," he announces as he stretches a hand up to the boat to help me out.

My cheeks warm at the way he calls me "little lass." It's an endearment, like "my love" or "baby." Surely, he doesn't mean it like that?

"I usually just fish off the boat," he explains as I place my hand in his, "but I wanted to show you this place. Something told me you would appreciate it."

"It's beautiful," I breathe as he helps me from the boat.

I look around the cave as I step down. Sunlight bathes the shore right outside where we're docked, and when I look up, I see the beautiful rock formations of the cave.

Of course, my clumsy ass stumbles whenever I look up and try to move at the same time. I should know by now that I can't walk and chew gum simultaneously, much less move and look up at the mouth of a cave.

But Sean doesn't let me fall. Instead, two strong arms wrap around my back and pull me flush against a hard, perfectly toned chest. "Careful there, lass," his deep voice rumbles right against my ear.

Sweet baby Jesus, it's even more mesmerizing than I imagined it would be. A tremble passes through my body, and I know he must feel it because I'm pressed completely against him.

His hands slide down to my waist and rest there. He doesn't release me, and when I look up at him, his eyes are blazing down at me.

"Sean." I say his name for the first time, my voice shaky and breathless. My head is spinning at his nearness, and I don't know what I'm supposed to do. Part of me is saying I should step back and pull away, but another part is yelling, Don't you dare! Enjoy every moment of this while you can!

I finally listen to the sensible part of my brain and pull away from him. His arms fall from my waist, and he runs a big hand through his tangled mass of hair. He's disheveled, with his bare chest and wild hair. He looks like an untamed beast, and I force myself to stop gawping at him.

"What is this place?" I finally manage to ask with genuine curiosity.

"It doesn't have a name," he answers as he walks over to the mouth of the cave and bends down at the shoreline. "It's just a place I love to come to. I've always found it peaceful and beautiful."

He plucks a white flower from one of the sand dunes at the mouth of the cave and heads back over to me. "Here."

I take it, gingerly stroking the soft petals. "Thank you. It's so pretty." I can't help the blush that stains my cheeks. A man has never given me flowers before. This may not be an expensive bouquet but knowing that he picked it just for me makes it special.

"What kind of flower is it?" I glance at him to find his gaze trained on me, an unreadable expression on his face.

"The white rose of Scotland, also known as Scots rose or Burnett rose. They grow more abundantly here than anywhere else I've found."

My eyes scan the vicinity and take in all the beautiful white roses nestled among the limestone heath. The blossoms are plentiful here, and my heart warms at the thought that he brought me somewhere like this.

He takes the flower back from me and breaks the stem so that it's shorter before sliding it behind my ear. My breath catches as his fingers trail along my jaw to my chin before he finally drops his hand. I fight the urge to nuzzle against his hand like a pampered cat.

He clears his throat and looks out over the water. "You ready to catch some fish, lass?"

My naturally curious nature takes over. I love learning new things, and this will be something new for me. "I've never even held a fishing pole in my hand," I tell him.

He raises an eyebrow at me. "Well, today's your lucky

day, lass. I'll teach you all you need to know about holding a rod."

He winks at me, and my breath catches as my cheeks blaze. Is he purposefully making sexual insinuations, or do I have a dirty mind? I don't see how I could have a dirty mind, though. I'm a virgin. Hell, maybe that's what my problem is. I'm hypersensitive *because* I'm a virgin, and this man is making me horny as hell.

He chuckles at the look on my face and then swaggers over to the boat to pull out a couple of fishing rods. I watch as he deftly sets up each rod and then baits the hooks with a couple of worms.

He laughs when I wrinkle up my nose as he slips the slimy creatures onto the hooks. "Don't worry, lass. I'll always bait your hooks for you. You'll never have to get your hands dirty," he tells me before he walks over to the water and dips his hands in to clean them.

"It's not because they look all icky and slimy. What about the poor creatures? Doesn't it hurt them to be run through with a hook?"

Sean pauses as if he's never considered that before. "We could just fish with jigs if you'd prefer. Granted, fish will usually bite live bait better, but sometimes they'll bite an artificial jig."

Before I can answer one way or the other, he gently slips the worms off the hooks and then places them in the soil nearby. I don't know if they'll still live after being pierced, but the fact that he's willing to reconsider his actions softens something inside me. This man might be big and burly and look like some sort of untamed beast, but he's gentle and kind.

He hands me a fishing rod. His tone is serious as he vows, "I'll never use live bait again, lass."

I smile at him and take the outstretched rod. Did he just insinuate that he would stop doing something to please me? I can't believe he's willing to change the way he does things because he doesn't want to upset me. I don't point out that we're going to be hurting fish if we catch them because he might offer to swear off fishing forever, and that's his vocation.

"Here." He moves up behind me. "Let me show you how to cast."

His big arms wrap around me from behind. I'm completely enveloped in him, and his scent teases my nostrils. He smells like citrus and the sea and something decidedly masculine, making me giddy and lightheaded.

"Alright, you hold this line down, and pull your arm back like this." His voice is right in my ear as he leads me through the motions.

I watch as my line goes sailing out into the water further than I'd ever be able to cast it on my own.

He stands behind me for a beat longer than is necessary, his chest expanding against my back. Is he breathing me in like I am him?

The tension crackling between us is palpable. I clear my throat. "So, how long have you been a charter guide?"

My question breaks the trance, and he immediately steps back. "Pretty much my entire life." He retrieves his rod and casts it out into the ocean with a smooth flick of his wrist. "What about you, lass? What do you do?"

"Well, nothing yet," I admit. "I just graduated high school, and I'm supposed to go to college when I go home."

He frowns. "And where is home, lass?"

"America," I tell him softly, my stomach already dropping at the thought of going back.

His frown deepens, and he jerks on his fishing rod violently. He glances over at me, and his eyes soften as he tells me, "I knew you were smart." His voice is filled with pride that warms me from the inside out.

"So, what do you plan on majoring in, little lass?"

I frown before I answer. "Accounting."

Sean doesn't miss a beat. "But you're less than thrilled about that."

I blink, surprised at his perceptiveness. "I..." my voice trails off as I consider what to tell him. "Accounting is a sensible career."

"But it's not what you really want to do," he immediately surmises.

"I..." I try again before shaking my head no.

"If you could do anything you wanted, what would you do, lass?"

That moniker warms me again, and something about it prods me to tell him the truth. "I love to write."

He smiles at me before he tells me gently, "So write." He says it like it's simple.

I shake my head. "It's not that easy."

"Why not?" The concern in his eyes is genuine. His green eyes are warm and focused completely on me.

"Because my mom wants me to go into accounting. She had to scrape by working minimum wage jobs her entire life as a single mother. She wants better for me. And writing isn't a stable occupation." I release a hollow laugh. "They didn't coin the phrase 'starving artists' for nothing."

I grip my pole more firmly. "I'm good with numbers. I would be good at accounting, and I'd always be able to find a job in that line of work. It's the smart, sensible thing to do."

I glance across at Sean and find his gaze still trained on me. I don't know who I'm trying to reassure about my career choice—me or him.

Sean nods his head slowly before his deep voice rumbles out, "But will you be happy?"

I bite my lip. "I think that's the first time anyone has ever asked me that," I admit in a whisper.

Tears spring to my eyes when I realize it's the truth. My own mother has never asked me what would make me happy, yet here is Sean—a man I just met and barely know—asking me that very question and looking at me as if he truly cares about my happiness.

There's the crux of the problem, uttered in his deep Scottish brogue.

Will I be happy?

chapter
six

Sean

Seeing tears glistening in Ivy's eyes is my undoing. I smash my rod into the sand and rush over to her. I take her rod from her hand and stick it quickly into the sand before I turn to her and pull her into my arms.

"Shh, shh, don't cry, little lass."

She buries her face in my chest, and although she's not making a sound, her shoulders are shaking, and her tears wet my bare chest.

"Fuck, Ivy, lass." I feel so helpless. Seeing her cry is like a knife through my heart.

"I'm sorry," she mumbles as she lifts her head and

starts wiping her eyes. "I don't know what came over me."

I gently push her hands away from her face and take over the task of wiping her tears away. She looks up at me, and her shimmering blue pools nearly knock me over. Before I even register what I'm doing, I have her face cupped in my hands. Her lips part and I'm a goner.

I kiss her, pouring all the emotion I feel for her into that kiss. When she begins to respond, I slide my hands into her hair and deepen the kiss. I glide my hands down her back and clutch her close to me just as the fishing pole snaps against my leg. Ivy feels it too because she pulls back and looks up at me with wide eyes.

As much as I want to say fuck the fish, there's too much excitement in her blue orbs. I won't deprive her of this moment. It's always exciting when someone catches their first fish.

I snatch up the rod and press it into her hands, circling behind her and showing her how to reel in the fish. She smiles up at me, her blue eyes sparkling innocently. It's all I can do not to taste her sweet lips again, especially when I see that they're still swollen and pink from our kiss a few moments ago.

I force myself to release my arms from around her, letting her reel in her fish on her own so it's truly her catch.

"What kind of fish is it?" she asks excitedly as she holds up the line.

I look it over. "Looks like pollock." I chuckle at the look of pride on her face.

"Is it a keeper?" she asks hopefully.

"Oh, it's a keeper," I murmur, my gaze focused on her. I want her so badly that my whole body aches. It's more than a physical yearning. I want to hold her and hear every thought in her head.

I take the fish off the hook for her and throw it in the cooler. "You want to keep going?" I ask her with a grin, but I already know the answer.

She's got the fishing fever in her eyes as she nods her head. "You bet!"

I chuckle as I check the jig on her hook and help her cast again. She might be able to cast the rod on her own now, and I suppose I should let her try, but I want an excuse to feel her in my arms again.

We go back to fishing, neither of us speaking of the kiss. We cast glances at each other, smiling when our gazes tangle. I'm not old, but Ivy makes me feel young, more alive.

She tells me about her Aunt Sadie and what it's like to live in the States, and I tell her about Deacon and life here in Scotland. Even though we come from vastly different places, we have a connection that pulses with promise. I can't say we have a lot in common other than we both love the water, and I'm teaching her to love fishing. She's so much smarter than me. I never cared about school, but my chest puffs with pride when I hear that my little lass graduated top of her class and got a full-ride scholarship to college.

We are opposites in many ways. She's American, and I'm Scottish. She's tiny, and I'm huge. She's the intellectual type, whereas I'm an outdoorsman who lives by my wits. Even so, everything inside me feels right with her. She's the other half of me I never knew I was missing.

I tell her every funny story I know just to see her eyes crinkle up and hear the gentle peals of her laughter. I don't notice how much time has passed until I suddenly see the storm clouds rolling in. I frown as I look up at them. They're moving in way too fast. I checked the weather forecast before I agreed to come out today–something every charter guide pays scrupulous attention to–and nothing was forecast. Still, the weather here in Scotland can be unpredictable at the best of times, and it's not uncommon for one to creep up at a moment's notice. I know the signs, and I'm usually good at recognizing them. There's a subtle change in the air, a certain look to the skies.

But I've been so wrapped up in Ivy that I missed all the signs, and now I can tell by how quickly the skies are darkening that it'll be too dangerous to try to make it back to the mainland.

"Should we go?" Ivy sends me a worried glance as thunder rumbles in the distance.

I reel in my line and motion for her to do the same. "I'm afraid not. The storm is moving in too quickly. We need to pack up and seek shelter in the cave."

Ivy doesn't protest. She simply does as I say, reeling in her line and helping me take the fold-up chairs I got out for us earlier back to the boat.

Although we work quickly, the storm is moving in rapidly. By the time we get everything packed up, we're both soaked.

Lightning cracks too close for comfort, and the echoing roll of accompanying thunder sounds a moment later. I motion for Ivy to go to the cave.

She shakes her head and yells over the downpour. "Not without you! I can help!"

Her insistence is both touching and frustrating. "I'm right behind you!" I yell back.

The wind is picking up. I have to make sure the boat is tied off securely so it's not pulled away from the shore or we'll really be up shit's creek when the storm passes. I don't know about Ivy, but I don't have my phone on me. Even if she has hers, there's no cell signal out here. That's why I never bother to bring my phone with me on the water.

"Go!" I insist.

But she's stubborn and helps pull the rope to bring the boat even closer to shore where I can tie it more securely.

I make quick work of it in my haste to get her out of the rain. I can take the chill of Scotland's storms, but Ivy has been huddled up in a jacket all day, despite the shorts she's wearing. My little lass is used to a warmer climate, and she's going to be shivering in no time.

I finally get the boat fixed up to weather the storm. I grab the cooler in one hand and take her hand in the other. We run to the mouth of the cave and make it inside just as another flash of lightning strikes on the beach.

I curse myself internally, calling myself every name under the currently absent sun for not keeping a closer eye on the weather and putting my Ivy in danger.

When we're finally all the way in the shelter of the cave, I sit Ivy down on one of the large rocks sticking out of the sand. Even though the storm has darkened the skies, it's not nighttime yet, so there's still enough light in the cave for us to see by.

My throat goes dry when I see Ivy's wet hair pressed

against her cheeks. Her clothing is clinging to her skin, showing off every curve of her body. I stare at her, trying to keep myself under control because every muscle in my body is primed to pounce on her and mount her like an animal.

She shivers, and the visible realization that she's cold snaps me back to my senses. I head over to the pile of wood I have gathered in the base of the cave for emergencies like this. Granted, I've never had to use any of the wood to build a fire, but I'm glad I had the foresight to take the precaution.

My woman is cold, so I'm going to build her a fire. The task gives me something to do to distract me from my lust—not entirely, but it keeps my hands busy so I don't act on it.

I square my jaw. I need to take care of my little lass. After all, it's my fault we're in this situation.

chapter
seven

Ivy

I probably look like a drowned kitten. I try my best to wring out my dripping wet hair, but Sean doesn't even bother with his. He busies himself gathering wood for a fire, though I don't know how he plans on lighting it unless he knows how to rub two sticks together like they do in the movies.

When he rummages around in a small, square metal tin, pulling out some matches and dry leaves, I realize he's completely prepared for a situation like this. I wasn't overly panicked when I saw the storm coming in. Somehow, I instinctively knew that Sean would take care of us.

He starts a fire just as competently as everything else he's put his hand to today. I can't help but wonder if his hands are competent in other ways...

"Ivy." His deep voice grabs my attention. He comes to stand before me, his green eyes dark with concern as he looks at me. "You're shivering, lass."

I hadn't noticed how cold I was, but now that he's pointed it out, I'm super aware of it and can't stop my teeth from chattering.

"Come here." He takes my hand and leads me over to the fire. The warmth emanating from it is an instant relief, but it's going to take me forever to get warm in my soaking wet clothes.

Sean must think the same thing. "You'll dry faster if you take off your clothes."

I glance up at him, my cheeks turning pink at his suggestion. Is he saying that because it's true or because he wants to see me undressed?

He clears his throat, but his voice is deep and husky when he adds, "At least down to your underwear. Those jean shorts and that jacket are heavy, so they'll take a while to dry.

I'm glad I wore a bikini underneath my clothes because it won't be as intimate as my underwear. A bikini is a bathing suit, right? So, it should be socially acceptable.

I strip down to my pink bikini, and I instantly feel warmer without the soggy clothing weighing me down. Sean stares at me for a beat before he takes my wet clothing from me and lays it out on a rock near the fire to dry.

Good lord, if I thought it would be less intimate to wear a bikini in front of him, I was wrong. With the way his gaze is roving over me, I feel more exposed than ever. I fight the urge to cross my arms over myself, especially when my breasts and the area between my legs suddenly feel fuller and more sensitive than normal.

"You hungry?" Sean asks as he turns to the cooler and pulls out the fish we caught.

My stomach growls in reply.

Sean smiles. "Good thing you caught us dinner."

I watch with interest as he cleans the fish with just a pocketknife and then puts it on a stick to cook it over the fire.

"You're a survivalist," I note.

Sean looks up at me with a half-smile. "Yeah, I guess I am. I've always been the outdoorsy type. I want to be able to take care of myself if I ever get stranded somewhere." He motions around us. "Like now."

He pauses, giving me an apologetic look. "Sorry about that, by the way, lass. I should've paid more attention to the incoming weather."

"It's okay," I tell him as I settle down on the rock beside him. "I feel safe with you."

"You do?" he asks in surprise.

I blush at my admission, but I'm not sorry it slipped out. "Yeah."

He smiles at me—a smile that makes me wish I didn't have to go home. I remember the way he kissed me, and I wonder if he just wants a fling or something more.

But it doesn't matter, I remind myself. I have my scholarship, and my week will be up before I know it.

That thought sobers me, and I look away from him. I can't get attached to Sean, though it would be so easy. He's perfect, with his sure manner, cover-model physique, and dazzling smile.

"When do you have to go back?" he asks softly as if he knows where my mind has gone.

"At the end of the week," I tell him vaguely, not wanting to talk about it. The air between us grows heavy, so I change the subject. "You should teach survival classes or something. You're so good at all this. People would pay money to learn the kinds of skills you have."

"You think?" His chest swells with pride, his eyes taking on a glimmer of excitement.

The sight makes me smile. "Definitely." I'm not lying. He'd be great at teaching stuff like that. "You could do it in addition to your charter trips."

His eyes dim as he turns the fish. "Maybe someday, if I ever start my own business, lass."

I wonder what's holding him back, but I don't ask. I don't want to pry or make him uncomfortable if it comes down to finances because I know what that's like.

It turns out I don't have to ask him because he volunteers the information.

"I would love to run my own charter business one day. I have so many ideas." He goes on to tell me about some of them, and it's obvious by the animated way he speaks that this is something he's thought about long and hard.

"I think you'd be great at it," I tell him honestly.

He smiles at me, then quickly sobers. "Yeah, I know I would." He doesn't say it cockily but with quiet confidence. "I just have to figure out how to do it without upsetting Deacon."

I can't help but admire how loyal he is to his boss.

"I know so many great spots I could show people that have nothing to do with fishing. I've pitched my ideas to Deacon," he sighs heavily and shakes his head, "but I'm afraid he's stuck in his ways. This is just a job to him now. He doesn't have the passion for it that he once did, so he doesn't care about expanding."

I don't know what to say and don't want to offer him empty platitudes, so I ask him to tell me about some of the other cool places he knows about. His eyes are full of passion when he talks about the landmarks. He describes them so vividly that I can picture them clearly.

"You'd be a great writer. You have a way with description. I almost feel like I'm there," I tell him honestly.

His handsome face breaks into a grin. "You think so?"

I nod.

He chuckles and shakes his head. "Well, thanks for the vote of confidence, lass, but I'm afraid I'm nowhere near smart enough for all that. I was never good in school. I just have a love for the land."

"You love your homeland," I note wistfully.

"Aye," he agrees. "There's no place like Scotland."

Maybe it makes me a traitor to my country, but I have to agree. This place is so beautiful, and I already feel more tied to it in my short time here than I ever have to my birthplace. Maybe Aunt Sadie is right, and there's something about Scotland being in our blood because I can see myself living here forever with no regrets.

We fall into a companionable silence as Sean finishes cooking the fish before handing one to me. The storm continues to rage beyond the cave and I hope Aunt Sadie isn't worrying too much that I'm not back yet. I glance up at Sean. I'm pretty sure Aunt Sadie knows I'm in good hands. She seemed to trust

Sean and would know he's prepared for situations like this.

I take a tentative bite of the fish. I'm not big on seafood but I'm pleasantly surprised when the smoky flavor hits my tongue. "Wow, this is good," I tell Sean. I close my eyes and moan as I take another bite, and then another, just savoring the food until nearly all of my fish is gone and my belly is full.

When I open my eyes, Sean is staring at me intently, his nostrils flared. My cheeks flush with embarrassment. I just made a complete pig of myself in front of the most handsome man I've ever met. What is wrong with me?

I stand up and walk a few paces away from him, looking out the mouth of the cave to see the storm still raging steadily. "Do you think we'll be stuck here all night?" I ask without turning around to look at him.

"Aye," he answers from right behind me, startling me so that I jump. His hands on my shoulders settle me. "You're shivering again. Are you cold, lass?"

Goosebumps rise across my flesh at his touch. "A bit," I answer honestly.

"Come back by the fire," he urges.

I readily obey and he settles us so we're sitting on the ground, our backs against the rock behind us. He opens his arm to me in invitation. I just stare at him, my heart thudding in my ears.

"I don't have any dry blankets," he explains, his voice low, "but body heat will help keep you warm."

I settle wordlessly into his side, and he wraps his arms around me, holding me close against him. He's so warm, like a big bear, and I wonder how someone can give off so much heat. Maybe it's not him. Maybe it's me. I'm burning with nerves and elation and so many other emotions that I can't dissect them all. Being wrapped up in Sean's arms like this is overwhelming. It feels so good yet disturbing at the same time.

His hands rub up and down my arms. "Better?" he asks huskily.

I tilt my head up to look at him. Biting my lip, I nod, suddenly unable to speak. I'm afraid that if I do, I'll confess how good it feels to be in his arms.

His eyes trail over my face, darkening as they fall on my mouth where I'm worrying the flesh. I instantly release my lip from my teeth, and his eyes flit up to capture mine.

"Fuck, Ivy, I can't take it anymore," he growls, right before his mouth crashes down on mine.

He kisses me deeply, hungrily, and my mind short-circuits from all the thoughts flying through my head.

This can't go anywhere. I have to return home to the States in less than a week.

But Sean's lips gliding across mine feel too good. His

tongue slipping inside my mouth sends shockwaves pulsing between my legs.

The sensible side of me tells me to stop this, but the other side of me–the side I keep locked away, the side that wants to be a writer and travel the world and do what *I* want to do instead of what my mother wants–tells me that this could work. But even if it doesn't, I can have this moment. If I end up being a fling for this gorgeous man, it'll be a happy fling.

But will I be happy?

Sean asked me that question earlier, and I didn't have an answer then. But I do now.

Yes. I'll be happy to let Sean do whatever he wants to me.

So, I melt against him, silently giving myself over to him completely.

This one week is mine, so I'm going to make the most of it. I'm going to think of what I want for a change.

And right now what I want is Sean.

chapter
eight

Sean

She's so beautiful. I'm not strong enough to resist the siren call of her lips, and when she melts into me, it's like I've died and gone to heaven. Her submission is a greater rush than reeling in the biggest fish in the oceans. I've never done drugs before, but I'm certain having Ivy in my arms is more potent than any mood-enhancing substance.

She might be a tiny thing, but she's got subtle curves in all the right places. I've been permanently hard since she stripped down to that little pink bikini that shows off her shapely legs and her round buttocks.

"Do you have any idea how breathtaking you are?" I

ask her in between kissing her lips, her cheeks, her eyes. I kiss her all over her face like a man worshiping an idol. I'm revering her, pouring every bit of passion I feel for her into my kisses. And it's still not enough. It will never be enough with her. I'll always want more. More of her. More of Ivy. More of my little lass.

She presses her hips against me, her movements unpracticed. It's obvious she's not experienced, and damn if that doesn't make me even wilder with need.

But I force myself to calm down long enough to make sure this is what she wants before I'm too far gone. I place my hands on her hips, stilling them and she lets out a little whimper, her eyes hooded and her pretty lips swollen from my kisses. She looks so damn beautiful, I could die a happy man right now.

"Are you sure, Ivy? Because once I start, I'm not sure I'll have the strength to stop, little lass."

Her eyes flutter up at me. Her cheeks are flushed, and her hair has dried into messy, beachy waves. She looks utterly fuckable, and I've never wanted anything in my life more than I want her at this moment. I'd sell my soul for just one more kiss—let alone the pleasure of sinking inside her tight virgin heat.

"I'm sure, Sean." She takes her lip between her teeth and worries it. "But I've never done this before..." she trails off, looking away from me like she's ashamed.

I blow out a breath and damn near fall to my knees at her confirmation of what I already suspected. *Mine.* She'll be all mine. No one else will ever claim her. Why in the world she thinks this would displease me is beyond me.

She lifts her eyes to me warily like she thinks I'm going to change my mind now that I know she's a virgin. Sweet Jesus, she truly has no idea how a man's mind works, does she?

I gently grip her chin and turn her to face me. "Being a virgin is a good thing, lass."

"You're not disappointed?" Her eyes are wide and vulnerable.

The place in my heart that she's already claimed grows larger as she notches herself even deeper in there.

I cup her jaw and stroke my thumbs along her cheeks as I let out an incredulous chuckle. "Of course not. I'm happier than you could ever understand."

She blinks. "Really? Why?"

"Because it means you'll be completely mine." I mean to say it gently, but the words come out more like a growl as the last thread of my control snaps. I can't hold back any longer. I've been holding myself back all day, and it's finally taken a toll on me. This is a battle I can't win, don't want to win.

I kiss her again, marveling at how she tastes like milk

and honey, so deliciously sweet. I can't get enough of her. I kiss her until we're both breathless before I finally force myself to pull my lips from hers.

She lets out a whimper of protest, but I shush her by kissing her neck and collarbone. "Shush, little lass. As much as I love your lips, I have the rest of this beautiful body to worship, and other lips to kiss."

I give her a wicked grin and her cheeks flame as she gasps at my insinuation. I don't know if she realizes it or not, but I'm deathly serious. My mouth is watering in anticipation of tasting the sweet treat between her thighs.

But first I make my way over the gentle swell of her breasts, pushing the triangles of her bikini top to the side to expose her rosy nipples to my hungry mouth. She's responsive to my every kiss and touch. She throws her hands around my neck, her head falling back on a moan as I feast on her breasts.

I make it a point to kiss every inch of her skin, ignoring the pain of my arousal in favor of feeding her pleasure. This is my little lass's first time, and I'm deter-mined to make it good for her.

When I finally drop to my knees in front of her and undo the ties on the sides of her bikini bottoms, exposing her pretty mound to me, I want to weep at the sight. "Swear to god, I've never seen anything so pretty, Ivy," I tell her before I go in for my first lick.

She fists her hands in my hair as I go to town on her. I groan at the taste of her sweetness. I can't decide what tastes better, her pussy or her lips. I know one thing. I'll happily spend the rest of my life tasting both to find out.

She's so tight I can barely work one finger inside her. Her hands pull at my hair as I struggle to push another finger into her, knowing that she needs to be prepared to take me.

"Sssh, little lass. As you can see, I'm not a small man by any means, so we've got to get you ready for me." I'm sure she knows from my bulge pressed against her stomach when I was kissing her that I'm just as big there as I am everywhere else.

"Sean..."

Her breathy moan sends a rush of potent desire crashing through me. I'm not going to last much longer without busting, and I'm not even inside her.

She whimpers my name again as I continue to tease her with my tongue while gently stroking my fingers in and out of her, taking care not to break the barrier of her innocence. No, she's going to remain a virgin until I seat myself deep inside her and join us together as one.

She looks so motherfucking sexy with her long

blonde hair wild about her face, her skin flushed, and her eyes unfocused. She screams my name, and I feel my sex jerk in response as I stain the inside of my swimming trunks with a stream of precum. I'm so full and ready and hearing her scream my name as she orgasms all over my fingers and face is more than enough to send me toppling over the edge.

I lap up all her cream until her legs are shaking, and then I push her down so that she's laying spread out over the large rock by the fire. All I can do is stare at her for a moment, marveling at her naked curves. I don't deserve this woman. She's too beautiful. Too perfect, and I can't believe she's offering that perfection to me.

I quickly shuck my swimming trunks. Her eyes widen when she takes in my size. It doesn't help that she's got me so worked up that I'm harder and bigger than I've ever been in my entire life.

"Are you sure...?"

"It'll fit, lass. I promise," I rush to reassure her. "Do you trust me?"

She turns those beautiful cerulean eyes on me and nods. That small gesture of trust humbles me. I'm shaking with more emotion than I thought myself capable of. She looks so innocent and sexy, it's enough to make a man cry.

"I promise I'm going to take care of you," I vow as I

settle myself between her legs and slowly begin to push into her slick channel. Holy fuck! I close my eyes for a moment to savor the sensation of her tight heat gripping me and to stop myself from spilling prematurely.

She clutches onto my shoulders, tensing at my invasion.

"Relax, Ivy." I coax, planting gentle kisses along her shoulders and neck. Only when I feel her muscles soften do I rear back and plunge deep inside her in one hard thrust.

She screams, and I curse. I hate myself for hurting her, but she's so fucking tight and wet and hot I can hardly see straight.

I hold still inside her for as long as I can, every muscle in my body taut with the effort. "Are you okay, lass?" I finally manage to ask her through gritted teeth.

She licks her lips, her face flushed. "I think so. It doesn't hurt so much anymore."

I drop soothing kisses all over her cheeks. "I'm sorry, lass. So sorry. So sorry I hurt you. It's tearing me up inside knowing I did."

She smiles at me shyly. "It's okay. It was more like a sharp pinch."

I pause a moment longer, gently stroking my fingers along her arms and chest, savoring the way she trembles at my touch while I let her get accustomed to my size. When I feel like I'll die if I don't move, I test her readiness by pulling slightly out and pushing back in.

She moans, her eyelashes fluttering closed as she lifts her hips to me. "That feels so good."

Her voice is husky and so sexy it's all I can do to keep from spilling inside her. "Fuck, Ivy, I can't hold back any longer," I warn her as every muscle in my body strains.

"It's okay," she assures me, wriggling beneath me and causing me to slide deeper inside her. "Take me."

Her words unleash something inside me. I begin stroking in and out of her, groaning at the sweet sensation. There's nothing else at this moment but her and me and the sweet glide of our bodies.

"Tell me you're mine," I breathe against her lips, needing to hear her say the words.

"I'm yours," she says in between gasps and moans.

I kiss her to seal the deal. "Only mine," I prompt her, not knowing why I need more promises from her, just that I do.

"Only yours," she agrees.

"We're one, Ivy. You feel that?" I press my chest against hers so that our hearts are beating in tandem with one another. "Two hearts beating as one. I've never felt this close to anyone. You're special. You're different. You're *mine*. You understand, lass? You belong to me now. No one else is ever going to be inside you like this.

I'm not letting you get away from me now. You're taken, little lass. You hear me?"

I'm talking nonsense. She probably thinks I'm crazy, but I can't stop the flow of honesty pouring from my lips. I love this woman. I've loved her from the moment I first set eyes on her on the shores of the mainland. Knew she was meant to be mine. I'm claiming her now, and we'll never be apart after this. Never.

"Sean!" She gasps my name as I rut into her like a man possessed.

Every cell in my body is demanding I plant my seed in her. I'm aware we're not using protection, and I secretly hope she isn't on birth control because my primitive caveman is demanding I breed her. I need the entire world to see she's good and bred, that she's mine and only mine, and I'll kill any man who looks at her. The thought of planting my seed inside her is too much, and I can't hold back any longer.

I roar my release, shouting her name, chanting it like a prayer as I come inside her. I feel her quaking around me as she moans and calls out my name. We come together as one, her greedy womb sucking at my cock while I continue to spill inside her until she's overflowing, my essence leaking all over both of us.

I pull out of her gently, not even bothering to clean

us up. I'm too exhausted, and the laxness of her body tells me she is too.

I lay back on the large rock and pull her on top of me so that her tiny body is sprawled atop mine. "Sleep, little lass," I tell her as I place a kiss on the top of her head and wrap her in my arms.

I don't have to tell her twice. She goes out like a light, drifting off to sleep, her head burrowed in the crook of my neck.

I stroke my hands over her bare back, our bodies warmed by the fire. I'm utterly content as her precious weight rests on me while she sleeps. Nothing has ever felt so right.

I meant what I said. I'm never going to let her go now. I can't. Not after she gave herself to me so completely.

Ivy's wound herself into my heart and soul, and there's no way to get her out now short of killing me.

Ivy

I wake up on something hard and warm. When it moves up and down beneath me, I open my sleepy eyes to see it's Sean. I blush as memories of the previous night come crashing down on me.

"Good morning, little lass." That big chest rumbles beneath me.

I turn my head up to look into his face. He's smiling down at me tenderly, and his possessive words from the night before come flooding back.

"Good morning," I tell him shyly, though why I suddenly feel shy around him is beyond me. I mean, the man has seen me completely naked. He's been inside me and had me moaning and writhing and falling apart beneath him in pleasure. I think it's safe to say he's seen every part of me so there's nothing left to hide or be embarrassed about. And from what I remember, he was pleased with every part he saw, which fills me with giddiness and confidence.

He tilts my chin up with his hand and leans down to kiss me.

"Morning breath," I mumble, pulling away from him, mortified by the thought that I might gross him out.

He grabs my chin and pulls me gently back to him. "I don't give a fuck."

He presses a chaste kiss to my lips. I know he wants to deepen the kiss, but he doesn't as a show of respect for my boundaries. That knowledge causes me to throw caution to the wind, and I open my mouth and allow him to slip inside.

He fists his hands in my hair and groans into my mouth, and I feel him stiffening and lengthening between us. His hardness slides over my stomach, leaving a trail of moisture in its wake as he lifts my bottom and then settles himself at my core.

"Gotta have that sweet pussy again, little lass," he tells me before he slips gently inside.

I wince slightly at the soreness, but the pinch of pain

quickly turns to pleasure when he starts to move in long, lazy strokes inside me.

"Look at me," he whispers.

His emerald-green eyes glow with such tenderness it makes my heart hurt. I raise my hand to stroke his jaw, his beard coarse beneath my fingertips.

He covers my hand with his, holding my hip with the other as he continues to move inside me. "Ivy, lass," he swallows as if he's overcome with emotion, "I don't ever want to be parted from you. Anywhere you go, let me go too."

I blink back tears. I can't believe how close I feel to this man. Closer than I've ever felt to anyone. He gets me. He sees me, and he believes in me. He cares about my happiness.

"Ivy," he prompts me. "Say something, love."

Love. Hearing him call me "love" makes my heart melt. "I want that more than anything," I confess softly.

He grabs the back of my neck and pulls my lips down to meet his as he picks up his pace, stabbing deeper inside me. I move my hips down on him, meeting him thrust for thrust as the pressure within us builds.

We gaze into each other's eyes as we move together. No words are needed. Our souls are speaking for us, saying what we can't put into words. And when our release crashes over us in waves and his liquid heat spills into me, I'm complete for the first time in my life.

———

I'm floating on cloud nine when we finally get back to the mainland. It's so sunny that you'd never know a storm raged through the night. The sun is glinting off the waves, and everything is vibrant and beautiful.

I'm buzzing with happiness. Sean sat me in the seat right beside him and held my hand the entire way back to the shore. He doesn't release it even when we pull into the dock and see the throng of people already waiting there to greet us.

Aunt Sadie, and Sean's boss, Deacon, are standing at the front of the crowd. Sean's hand reluctantly slips from mine when Aunt Sadie throws her arms around me and pulls me into a tight hug.

"I'm so glad you're okay, honey, but I knew you would be. You were safe with Sean." She winks at him.

He grins at her before giving me a heated look. "Always. She's always safe with me."

Aunt Sadie casts a discerning eye between the two of us. I swear she knows what happened between Sean and me. I feel like it's stamped all over my forehead.

"You must be exhausted and hungry," she says,

draping an arm around my shoulder. "How long has it been since you had something to eat?"

"Oh, Sean cooked us some fish over the fire last night," I'm quick to assure my aunt.

"Ivy caught the fish yesterday," Sean adds proudly. "She's a natural."

I blush at the pride in his eyes as he gazes down at me tenderly.

"Glad you're okay, man." Sean's boss claps him on his back, and Sean shrugs. "I've been caught out in worse."

"Didn't you see those storm clouds rolling in?" his boss asks him.

Sean casts a glance in my direction, a half-smile on his face. "I was a wee bit distracted."

I practically melt into a puddle when I hear him say "a wee bit." If the way his smile widens is any indication, he knows it too.

"Well, thanks for taking care of my niece," my aunt chimes in.

"Oh, I took real good care of her." Sean's still smiling, his eyes trained on me.

I look down, my face flaming, as I consider kicking him. Does he not realize how suggestive his words sound? One glance at him, and I see that he knows exactly what he's doing. His eyes are twinkling with amusement, and he has a shit-eating grin on his face.

Aunt Sadie smiles widely as she looks back and forth between us.

"I could really use a shower," I tell her. "Thanks for the ride," I say to Sean, my voice a little stiff. I'm not sure how we're supposed to act in front of other people. I know what he said back in the cave, but was it all talk in the heat of the moment?

"Any time, little lass," he says with a smirk.

My heart skitters in my chest as I turn to leave with Aunt Sadie.

Sean captures my hand and pulls me back. "Will I see you later, lass?" His voice is deep and his eyes are full of promise as he speaks close to my ear.

I just nod, my throat too tight to speak.

Sean chuckles and then presses his lips against mine right there in front of a beach full of people. It's a chaste kiss, but it leaves no doubt as to the nature of our relationship and answers the question of whether he's serious about us or not.

I look up into his twinkling eyes. The wind blows and tousles his hair. He's so gorgeous, my Scotsman.

"Yes, I'm very serious about us, lass," he whispers, letting me know he was reading my thoughts. "You need to go, little lass," his voice is like rich velvet against my ear as he warns me, "before I claim you again right here in front of all these people."

That place between my legs pulses at his words, and my mouth drops open. Before I can say anything, he straightens and walks away with his boss.

My legs feel like jelly, but somehow I get them to solidify enough to walk back to my aunt's house with her.

I wasn't lying when I told my aunt I could use a shower, but now I think I'll be needing a cold one.

Ivy

I have to give it to my Aunt Sadie. I half expect her to grill me about what went down between Sean and me on the walk back to her place, but she doesn't. Maybe she can tell I need time to process everything but I'm grateful she doesn't press me for information.

Instead, she chatters on about the real estate deal and how they finally closed on it. She talks about the celebration they had afterward, and how she texted me but figured I didn't have any cell signal since I never texted her back. She later realized I'd left my cell phone at her house and was worried when she came home and found out I wasn't there. When she discovered Sean hadn't returned either, she knew he'd keep me safe.

"I know things can happen, but Sean is a competent young man. If anyone knows what to do in an emergency, it's him. I was confident you were okay," Aunt Sadie says firmly. "Now your mother is another matter."

Her words finally break through the half-listening haze I was in. "Oh, no, Aunt Sadie!" My voice comes out in a whine. "You didn't tell Mom I was lost at sea?"

Please, please, please say she didn't tell Mom. She'll be worried to death and drive me crazy.

"Of course not!" Aunt Sadie looks offended that I would even think she would do such a thing. "I'm not an idiot, Ivy."

I relax, only to tense again when she continues, "I just told her you didn't come back on the boat but that I knew you were fine because the young man you were with is a competent outdoorsman with great survival skills."

"You what? Jesus, Aunt Sadie, I've got to call Mom. Like, right now!" I pick up my pace, nearly sprinting the rest of the way to Aunt Sadie's house.

Aunt Sadie hurries to keep up with me. Thankfully, she left her door unlocked, so when I get there, I barge right in. I'm quick to locate my phone, taking a few calming breaths so I'll sound normal before I hit Mom's name from my contact list.

"Ivy!" My mother's worried voice immediately comes over the line. "Oh, my god, Sadie told me what happened. Are you okay?"

"Yes, yes, Mom. I'm fine. Aunt Sadie kind of blew everything out of proportion. You know how she is."

Aunt Sadie comes in the door and huffs when she hears my comment. I wave her away, giving her an apologetic smile that hopefully soothes her ruffled feathers.

"But she said—"

"As you can hear, I'm fine. I promise," I interrupt my mom, not wanting to rehash everything. "It wasn't a big deal, and I wasn't harmed. I'm just tired and want to take a shower and relax."

"Well, okay, baby, but call me later? I've been worried sick about you."

My conscience pricks at me. My mom was worried sick about me, wondering if I'd drowned, and I was having the time of my life losing my virginity to the sexiest Scotsman I've ever known.

"Sure, Mom."

"You got a letter from your college yesterday," she tells me, her voice vibrating with pride. "I think it might have something to do with you getting CLEP credit for some of those math classes."

My good mood evaporates at the thought of college and going back to the States. Away from Sean. "You can read it to me later, okay?"

She agrees, making me promise again to call her later before I finally manage to get off the phone with her.

I head to the bathroom to take a shower, but my talk with my mother has killed the high I've been riding since last night. It's brought me crashing back down to earth. A ball of misery lodges in my stomach. I'm leaving at the end of the week. No matter how I feel about Sean, it simply won't work.

I turn on the water and stand under the warm spray as my thoughts tumble about in my head.

Could I stay here in Scotland with him? I don't want to be an accountant. I smile as I imagine being with Sean every day, but my smile slips when I consider the reality. He has his job as a charter guide, but what would I do? I can't ride around on his boat with him all day while he works. And if I'm honest with myself, I want to go to college. I got a full-ride scholarship, and I don't want to waste it. I just don't want to use it to major in accounting. I want to major in creative writing.

I chew on my lip as I finally turn off the spray and grab a towel.

Sean said he'd go wherever I go. Would he come to the U.S. with me? Then I remember the passion in his eyes as he talked about Scotland. Sean loves his homeland. He has dreams here. He has a life here. I can't ask him to give it all up for me. It wouldn't be fair to him. And what if he came to resent me for it one day? I couldn't bear that.

My heart aches at the thought of being without the one person who understands me. How can I live without him now that I know how amazing it is to be with him? Will I survive never being held tight in his arms again? My body aches to feel his arms around me right now.

I call my mom as I promised I would. I wish I could talk to her about everything I'm feeling, but I know she wouldn't get it, so I stay silent.

She was right. The letter was about me getting credit for math classes.

When I get off the phone with my mom, I sit on the edge of the guest bed in Aunt Sadie's house, tears streaming down my cheeks.

I know what I have to do, and it's going to break not one heart, but two.

Sean

I'm humming a merry tune and damn near skipping as I make my way over to Sadie's house. It's well into the evening, and I haven't heard from Ivy. I've been kicking myself all day for not getting her phone number before we parted this morning, and I waited as long as I could before I finally said to hell with it and took off to get my little lass. I haven't seen her since this morning, and it's been too long since I've had her in my arms.

I knock on the door, clutching the bouquet of white roses I picked for Ivy.

Sadie answers the door, her face falling when she sees

me. Her eyes flick to the bouquet in my hands, and she looks at me with pity in her eyes.

My stomach drops as I instantly sense that something's wrong. "Where's Ivy?" I ask without preamble.

Sadie shakes her head sadly before she walks over to the table in her foyer and picks up an envelope. She hands it to me and shakes her head. "I found this in her room."

I look down at the envelope. It has my name on it. "Where is she?" My voice is flat. A thousand emotions are tearing through me right now. Disbelief, panic, fear.

"When I called her, she was on her way to the airport."

I don't wait for her to explain further. I turn on my heel and sprint to the street, hailing the first taxi I see. "To the airport!" I yell at the man as I shove some cash in his face. "As quickly as you can get there, lad."

I hop into the backseat and tear into the letter, my eyes scanning it rapidly while my heart hammers away in my chest.

Dear Sean,

Last night was amazing. Giving myself to
you was beyond my wildest expecta-

tions. I'm sorry for leaving like this,
but I can't ask you to give up your
dreams for me, and I know you don't
want me to give up mine. It hurts me
to write this, but I have to tell you
how I feel. I don't want you thinking
I just bailed on you like you were a
meaningless fling. You mean so
much more to me than you'll ever
know. You'll always be in my heart,
and I know how crazy this must
sound since we only knew each other
a short time, but I love you, Sean. I'll
never forget you.

Forever your little lass,

Ivy

I'm breathing heavily by the time I get to the end
of Ivy's ridiculous note. Stupid, crazy, wonderful
girl. My heart is being ripped in two. What does she
think she's doing to me? She tells me she loves me, but
she's leaving me? Based on some noble notion of not
asking me to give up my dreams? Fuck, doesn't she

realize she *is* my dream? That without her, I'm nothing?

I suddenly realize that the reason I never went after my dream of owning a charter business before is because it wasn't really my dream. I've settled for less my whole life, but now I've found the missing piece. Ivy. I've been waiting for her. I never pursued my own business, but I'm sure as hell pursuing Ivy.

I ball the letter in my fist and stuff it into my pants pocket, barking at the driver to go faster. Something in my tone must spur him on because he begins to weave in and out of traffic like he's on the set of *The Fast and the Furious*. When he pulls up to the airport in record time, I jump out the door before the taxi has fully stopped.

I race into the terminal, yelling at the reception area to tell me which gate goes to the States. I'm running in that direction before the bewildered woman has the numbers out of her mouth, praying to whatever deity is out there that Ivy hasn't boarded the plane yet. If she has, I'll bust through security to get on the fucker and get her off. There's no way I'm going to allow her to leave like this. No way.

***

Ivy

I sit in the seats in front of the gate waiting for them to call for us to board the plane. My heart hurts, and I'm so stressed over my decision that my head hurts too. I keep chewing on my lip, wondering if I'm doing the right thing. I almost turned the taxi around three times to take me back to Aunt Sadie's, but in the end, I continued because isn't that what true love is? Sacrificing your wants for the good of the other person? This way, I'll go back to my mom, and Sean will be free to pursue his dream.

I traded my plane ticket for an earlier date. I'm all set to go, so why am I becoming more nervous the closer it gets to my flight being called?

"Ivy!"

I must be imagining things because I'm sure I hear Sean calling my name. Tears spring to my eyes. It's only been a few hours but I miss him so much I'm delirious with it.

"Ivy!"

I hear it again and my head snaps up. Maybe there's another woman named Ivy here? And a man who just sounds like Sean? Because that can't be *my* Scotsman. There's no way he could know where I am. I didn't tell anyone where I was...

I suddenly remember my Aunt Sadie calling me when I was in the taxi.

"Ivy Summers!"

I stand on shaking legs when I hear my full name. There's no doubt in my mind that it is *my* Scotsman. It's Sean. He's come for me.

Tears stream down my cheeks as Sean spots me and makes a beeline for me. The panic in his eyes is palpable, and it tears my heart out.

"Sean, what are—?"

Sean is on me in an instant, grabbing my shoulders and giving me a little shake, his eyes blazing down at me with equal parts fury and relief. He pulls a crumpled-up piece of paper from his pocket and shakes it. "What the hell is this, Ivy?"

I glance at the paper. I can't see the script, but I know it's the note I left him. "I didn't want you to think that I don't care."

Sean lets out an incredulous laugh and runs a hand through his hair, looking down at me as he shakes his head disbelievingly.

I'm crying in earnest now, the tears streaming down my cheeks, but I can't stop them. "I couldn't ask you to give up your dream, but I have to go back, Sean."

"Ivy." Sean cups my face and wipes my tears away

with the pads of his thumbs. "You don't have to ask me to give up my dream because *you're* my dream."

My brow furrows. "But what about the business you want to start? What about your homeland? You love it so much, Sean."

Sean shakes his head, his green eyes blazing down at me. "None of it means anything without you, Ivy. Did you not hear me when I asked you to let me go anywhere you go? I can't be without you, lass." His voice breaks. "It'll kill me. And if you are crazy, then we're crazy together because I love you too, little lass."

I let out a sob, and Sean pulls me close to his chest, wrapping his arms around me. All the emptiness I've been feeling since I left him melts away now I'm back in his embrace.

"If you want to go to the States and go to college, we'll go, lass. You're right not to turn down an opportunity like that. You have no idea how proud I am of you for being so smart. And when you get out of college, we'll go wherever you want to go. My dream is to be with you. I don't care where that is. I only have one stipulation."

I look up at him and sniff.

"You major in what you want to major in. Not what your mother wants you to major in. Not what you think I want. Not what anyone wants but you, little lass. I believe in you, Ivy, and I want you to be happy, and whatever you want to do, I'll support you every step of the way."

We're so wrapped up in each other that I've forgotten we're in an airport until I hear the murmurs and gasps of onlookers when Sean drops to one knee in front of me. My heart beats a mile a minute in my chest, and I cover my mouth with one hand when I realize his intention.

Sean takes my hand in his and kisses it reverently, his beautiful green eyes never leaving mine. "I don't have a ring on me at the moment, lass, but will you be mine forever? Will you let me go anywhere you go from this moment on? Will you take me for your husband?" He swallows nervously before he places another kiss on my palm. "Will you marry me, little lass?"

Tears are streaming down my cheeks in earnest now, and I let out a strangled laugh when I realize Sean just proposed to me in four different ways. My dear, sexy, wonderful Scotsman.

I must look a mess, but I don't care, and Sean doesn't either because he sees beyond the mess. He sees me. The real me. I'll never have to pretend to be anyone else with him.

I launch myself into his arms by way of an answer. He catches me and stands just in time for his lips to meet mine. We kiss each other deeply, and I hear "awing" and applause break out around us, but I don't care about any of that.

"Is that a yes, lass?" Sean raises an eyebrow when we finally break apart long enough to catch our breath.

"Aye," I answer with a jubilant smile. "'Tis."

Sean pulls me in for another kiss, and I wrap my arms and legs around him, clinging to my future husband as I kiss him with all the love I feel in my heart for him.

epilogue

Five years later

Sean

I glance over at my wife where she's laying in the boat, basking in the sun. My eyes rove over her little pink bikini. It's not the same one she wore five years ago when I met her. I long since destroyed that one tearing it off her body, but I've since bought her plenty more. It's my favorite thing to see her in since it reminds me of the day she fell in love with me. The day I made her mine.

I still can't get over what a lucky bastard I am.

Somehow, I ended up with the most amazing woman in the world. She's the mother of our two beautiful children, Timmy and Brianna. They're currently staying with their Aunt Sadie so Mommy and Daddy can have some alone time out on the boat. I know Sadie isn't their aunt, but that's what they call her, so we just go with it.

After I proposed to Ivy, we flew to the States together. By the time the plane landed, my proposal had gone viral, so her mother already knew about it. She welcomed me with open arms. She could tell I was the real deal and loved her daughter deeply. She and Ivy had a long talk, crying as they bared everything to one another.

Turns out, Ivy's mother just wanted her to be happy, but like any mother, she worried about her daughter's future. When Ivy explained to her mom what she really wanted to do, her mother saw the passion in her eyes and knew she'd succeed.

And succeed she has. Every book my little lass has released has been a bestseller. I'm so damn proud of her I could burst.

While she was in college, I worked at a local gym, giving survival training classes. It was great, but I missed being on the water. Ivy knew that, too. That's why, as soon as she graduated college, we came back here to Scotland. This land is in her blood as much as it is mine. There's nowhere else we'd rather be.

I finally realized my dream of owning my own charter business. Deacon ended up turning the business over to me. When I left to be with Ivy, he quickly realized he no longer had the passion for it. He ran it long enough for me to get back and then signed it all over to me. Said he was ready for early retirement. It worked out perfectly because now I can do what I love my way without stepping on my mentor's toes.

I slow as we near "our" cave, guiding the boat in just enough to get us out of the sun, but I don't dock. Instead, I drop anchor.

We won't need to get out of the boat for what I have planned.

I make my way over to where my wife is stretched out. She arches her back like a little kitten, and I drop a kiss on her lips before allowing my hands to skim over her warm body.

"Mmm," she murmurs against my lips as she arches her hips to meet my probing fingers.

I hiss out a breath when I feel how wet she is. "I think my wife is in need of her husband," I murmur against her lips. I'm already rock hard. I've been hard the entire ride over as I thought of everything I'm going to do to her.

"You think right, husband," she purrs, and that husky little voice of hers drives me crazy like it always does.

I had so many plans for how I was going to take her, but it's been so long since I've had her all to myself, I find myself pulling her up onto all fours as I rip her bikini bottoms roughly from her skin, revealing her perfectly round little ass.

She grips onto the side of the boat as I pull myself from my swimming trunks. I don't even take the time to pull them all the way down before I'm stuffing myself inside her in one fluid thrust.

"Christ!" I exclaim. She moans as she takes my thick girth inside her. "Still as tight as a virgin," I grit out.

"Just shut up and fuck me," she begs, and fuck if I can deny that kind of request.

I grab onto her hair and ram into her in quick thrusts. The boat rocks in tune with my rutting. I'd be embarrassed at how quickly I nut if not for the fact that my wife climaxes around me at the same moment I spill myself inside her.

I slump down onto her back, still buried inside her, and move her hair to the side to kiss the nape of her neck.

"Haven't you heard you're not supposed to rock the boat?" she teases me.

I laugh into the hollow of her neck. "The man who coined that phrase didn't have a tempting little lass on board with him."

Ivy laughs and pulls out from under me, pushing me down so I'm sitting and climbing on top of me to straddle me.

"You ready for round two?" she asks me with a raised eyebrow.

Her hair is wind-tousled, and I admire the freckles dotting her nose and cheeks before I kiss her simply because I can't help it.

"You know it. I'll never get enough of you, little lass," I tell her as I pull her down on my still hard length. I silently vow to have her pregnant again by the time this day is over.

Who knows? Maybe we'll be lucky enough to get caught in another thunderstorm.

THE END

Visit Emma's website to get a FREE book you can't get anywhere else: www.authoremmabray.com.